P9-DUU-274

Library of Congress Cataloging in Publication Data
was not available in time for publication of this book, but can be obtained from
the Library of Congress.
ISBN 0-688-10652-8   ISBN 0-688-10653-6 (lib.)
LC Number: 90-49816

LARGE AS LIFE

JULIA FINZEL

LOTHROP

Ladybug, ladybug, where are you going
On the back of a butterfly, hardly showing?

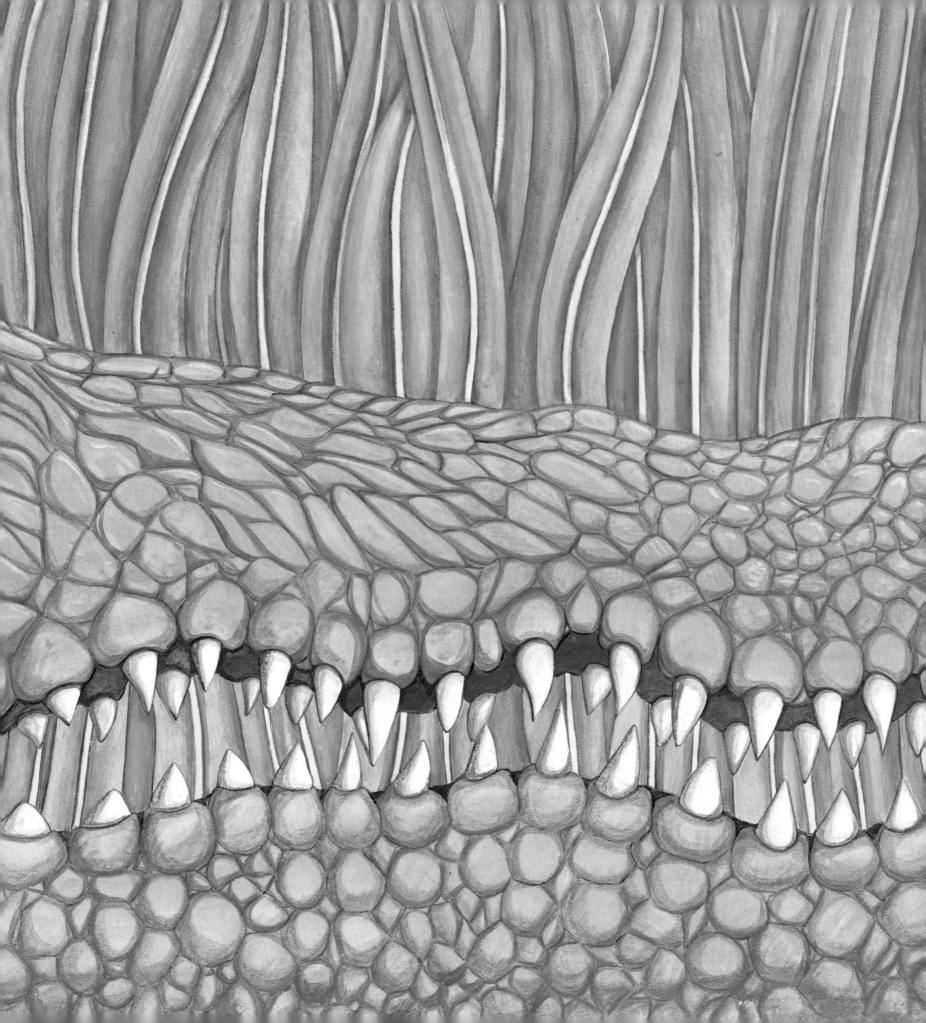

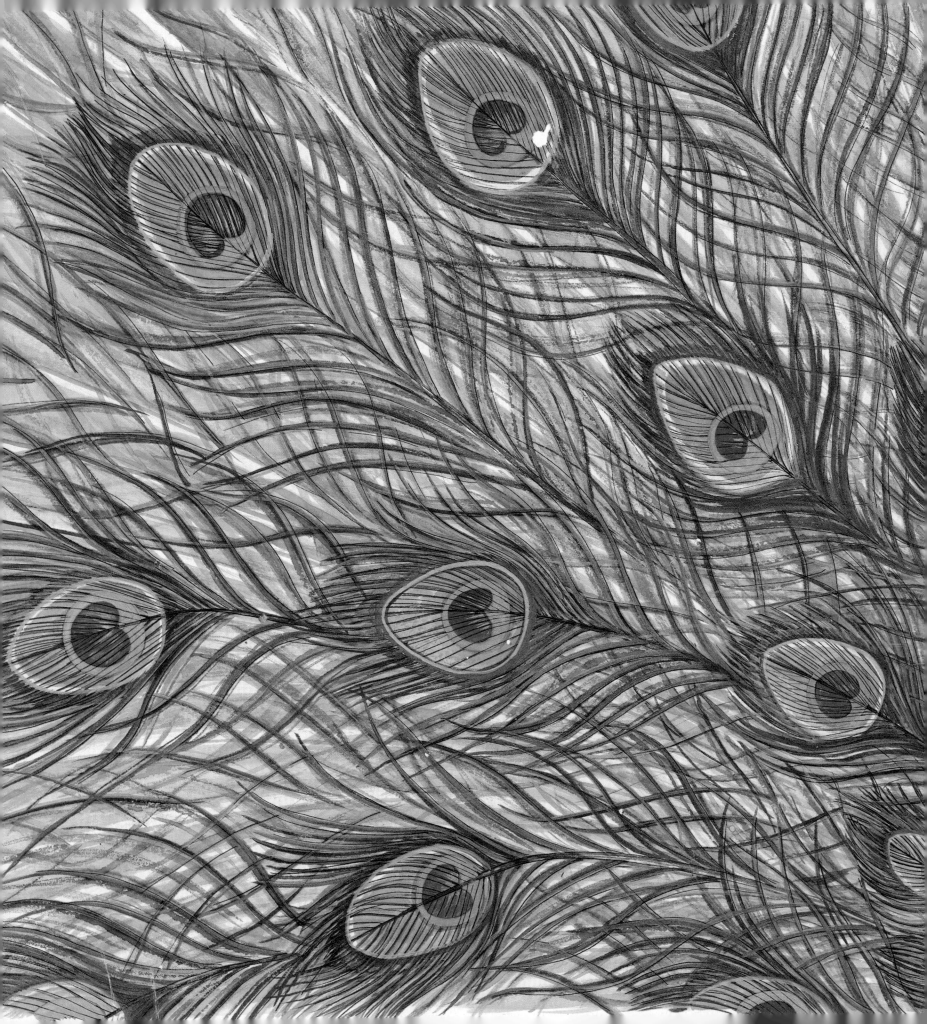

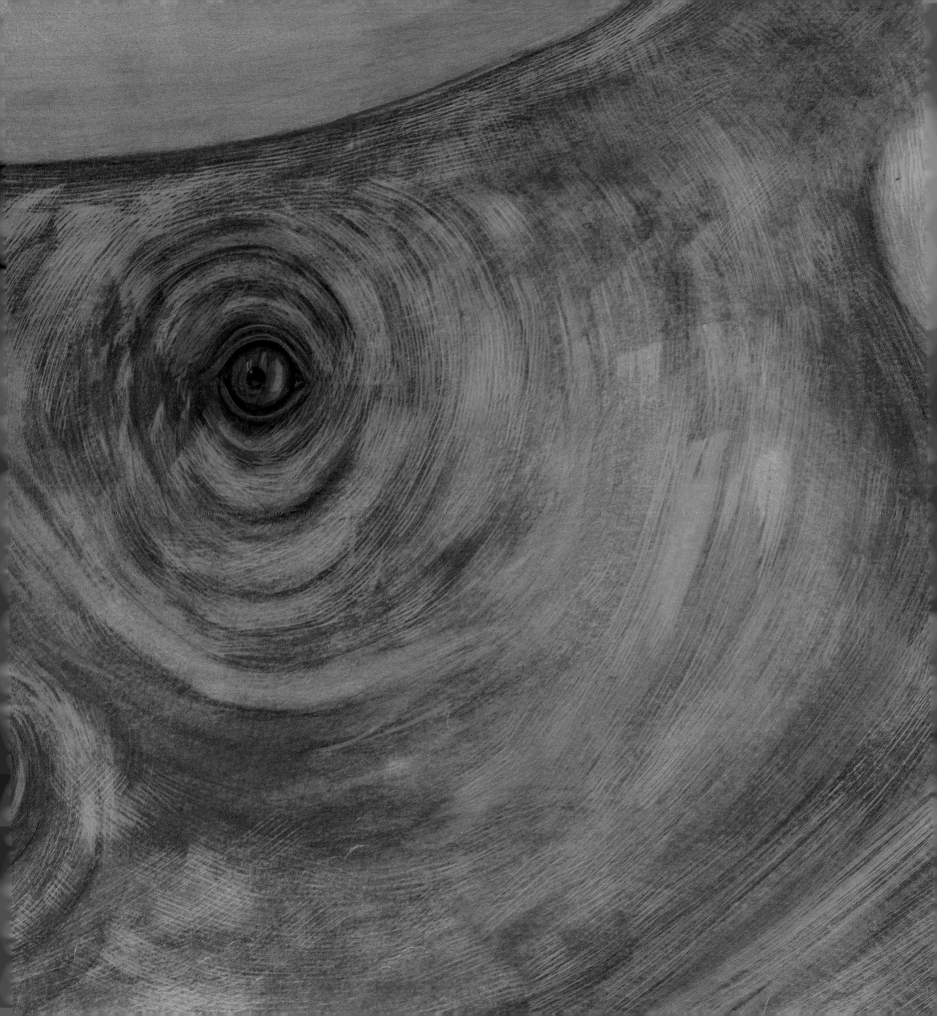

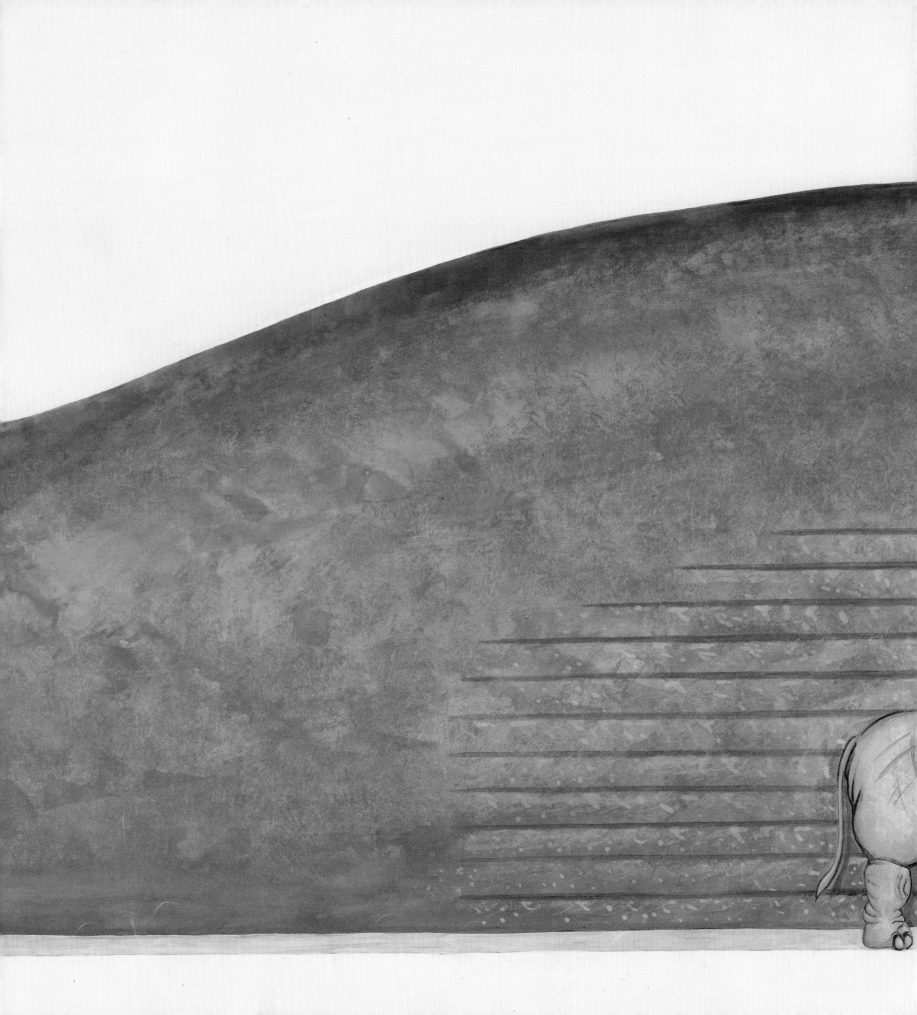

Ladybug, ladybug, where can you be?
In this giant parade, you're too small to see.

But no matter—near or far,
You're large as life wherever you are.